The Official Barney™ Annual

Published by
GRANDREAMS LIMITED,
435-437 Edgware Road, Little Venice,
London, W2 1TH

Contents

Art Director   Tricia Legault   *Contributing Illustrators*   Jay Johnson
Editorial Director   Guy Davis   Darrell Baker
Editor   Gayla Amaral   *Designers*   Joseph Hernandez
Contributing Authors   Mark Bernthal   Whitney Center
                          Guy Davis
                          Gayla Amaral

Your friends Barney, Baby Bop and BJ are having lots of fun while visiting a farm. Suddenly, they discover a big surprise! A mysterious, colourful egg has fallen from the sky like a shooting star! It's up to Barney and his pals to find out what's inside the egg. But first, our story begins on the farm...

My Friend Barney Had a Farm

(Sung to the tune of "Old MacDonald")

by Gayla Amaral

My friend Barney had a farm,
Super-dee-duper-dee-doo!
And on this farm he had a cow,
Super-dee-duper-dee-doo!
With a moo-moo here,
and a moo-moo there,
Here a moo, there a moo,
everywhere a moo-moo,
My friend Barney had a farm,
Super-dee-duper-dee-doo!

9

My friend Barney had a farm,
Super-dee-duper-dee-doo!
And on this farm he had a chicken,
Super-dee-duper-dee-doo!
With a cluck-cluck here,
and a cluck-cluck there,
Here a cluck, there a cluck,
everywhere a cluck-cluck,
My friend Barney had a farm,
Super-dee-duper-dee-doo!

My friend Barney had a farm,
Super-dee-duper-dee-doo!
And on this farm he had a horse,
Super-dee-duper-dee-doo!
With a neigh-neigh here,
and a neigh-neigh there,
Here a neigh, there a neigh,
everywhere a neigh-neigh,
My friend Barney had a farm,
Super-dee-duper-dee-doo!

Count With Barney

Can you point to 1 horse?
Well done!
Can you find 3 kittens,
3 goats and 7 chicks?
That's super-dee-duper!
What other animals do
you see?

Barney's Barnyard Maze

Barney and his friends discover an egg-citing surprise when they visit Greenfield Farm. Can you help Barney make his way around the farm to find the surprise? Can you find Barney's friends – Cody, Marcella, Abby, Agnes the horse, and Ralph the dog?

Moo-ve back to the path!

Duck back the other way!

Don't follow this flock!

16

Fun on the Farm!

Can you find Barney, BJ and Baby Bop in the barn?

18

Can you find a , 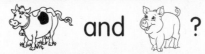 and ?

Look What Barney Found!

Barney and his friends Cody, Marcella and Abby have discovered a really big, colourful egg in the barn. It sure doesn't look like the kind of egg you'd usually find on the farm! Barney and his pals decide to visit Miss Goldfinch, a bird-watcher, who knows all about birds and eggs. "Maybe Miss Goldfinch will know something about this mysterious egg!" says Barney.

Barney Meets Miss Goldfinch

by Guy Davis

Barney has a new friend, she lives up in a tree.
Miss Goldfinch is her name, she's happy as can be!

Miss Goldfinch loves her birds
Who chirp and quack and cluck!
She even knows a swan
Who thought she was a duck!

Chirp, Chirp!
Tweet, tweet!
Cock-a-doodle-doo!
Gobble, gobble!
Quack, quack!
What bird sounds can you do?

Birds of every colour,
Birds of every feather,
They flock to Miss Goldfinch,
So happy together!

She's got peacocks and hens,
And a big cockatoo,
Two hot-pink flamingos
And a jaybird that's blue!

Cheep, cheep!
Caw, caw!
Whoo, whoo, whoo!
Peep, peep!
Cluck, cluck!
Wanna cracker, too?

She loves red robin
And her black crow that's cute,
And her wise little owl
Who really gives a hoot!

In her treehouse you'll find
A parrot who speaks words,
A gigantic condor,
And tiny hummingbirds!

She has toucans, penguins,
Some seagulls and a hawk,
And a regal eagle
Who really loves to squawk!

Remember, little friends,
Here's the Goldfinch Rule:
Treat nature with respect,
Be nice! Be kind! Be cool!

24

Always be a good egg,
And stay close to your nest,
Sing a song of good cheer,
Fly strong and fly your best!

Chirp, Chirp!
Tweet, tweet!
Cock-a-doodle-doo!

Cheep, cheep!
Caw, caw!
Whoo, whoo, whoo!

Peep, peep!
  Cluck, cluck!
    Wanna cracker, too?

  Gobble, gobble!
  Quack, quack!
What bird sounds can you do?

25

Watch the Birdies!

Help Barney match the birds that look exactly alike.

Feed the Birds

Help your child learn more about birds by making a birdfeeder. You will need these objects: wax paper, smooth peanut butter, pine cones, birdseed, and string.

- Place wax paper on the table.
- Spread a thin layer of smooth peanut butter on the waxed paper.
- Roll a pine cone in the peanut butter and then in the birdseed.
- Attach a string to the pine cone and hang it from a tree.

Children will love watching the birds eat from their special birdfeeder.

Follow That Egg!

Barney's friend, Miss Goldfinch, has figured out that a mysterious creature – a dream-maker – is inside the egg. But somehow, the egg gets lost! Where can it be? "There it goes!" shouts BJ, pointing at the birdseed salesman driving away. "It fell in the back of that truck!" "Follow that egg!" cries Barney.

Parade Fun!

"Where is the egg now?" asks Baby Bop. "Somehow it fell out of the truck and landed in this parade," answers Barney. "Look out!" cries BJ. "Here comes the marching band!" Suddenly, all three friends are swept up in the parade. "This is so much fun!" says BJ. "I love a parade!" laughs Baby Bop. "Let's all sing along!" says Barney.

Oh, When We March!

Music – Traditional
("When the Saints Go Marching In")
Lyrics by David B. Wolf

Oh, when we march,
It's so much fun;
It's fun to march with everyone,
Oh, it makes us feel real happy
When we march with everyone.

31

Oh, when we march,
We love the beat,
It's so much fun to lift our feet
As we're marching all together.
When we march, we love the beat.

Oh, when we march,
We hear the drum
As it plays its "Rum-T-Tum-Tum-Tum!"
Oh, we love to march together
When we hear the marching drum.

Oh, when we march,
We march somewhere;
Our marching takes us here to there.
Oh, we like to keep on moving
When we march from here to there.

35

Barney's Band

Help Barney lead the band to Baby Bop.

Music Hunt

Can you help Barney find 3 musical instruments?

Barney is still looking for the little lost egg. Somehow it's been handed over to someone at the circus! Where, oh where could it be? "We must find the egg," says Barney, "and return it to the farm before it hatches!"

A Circus Surprise!
By Mark Bernthal

Barney, BJ and Baby Bop ran into the big circus tent. Where could the egg be? There were so many places for it to be hidden! They all dashed off in different directions to look for the egg.

Suddenly, Baby Bop discovered the egg balanced on the tip of a seal's nose! "Oh no," she worried. "It might fall and break!"

But just then, with a flip of her head, the seal sent the egg flying across the tent. "Aye-yie-yie! Please catch that egg!" shouted BJ to the man on the flying trapeze.

41

Just as the man on the trapeze high above the crowd caught the egg, it slipped out of his hands and fell toward the ground. "Oh no!" shouted BJ. "The egg will be smashed!"

But it bounced off the safety net under the trapeze and sailed high in the air again.

The egg almost hit the ground, but a car full of clowns zipped past and it landed in a horn. Before BJ could catch up with the clowns, one of them honked his horn to make people laugh. "Honk!" went the horn, and out flew the egg again!

Barney was very surprised to see the egg roll through a lion's cage and be picked up by an elephant with its trunk! When the elephant trumpeted her loud call, she blew the egg across the bigtop into the hands of a juggler, who accidentally tossed the egg into the air toward a group of acrobats. "I hope they catch our egg!" shouted Barney. But it flew too high for them to reach.

As it was about to smash on the ground, Barney dived down, and safely caught the egg. "Whew! That was close!" said BJ. "It sure was," answered Barney. "Now we have to take the egg back to the barn quickly!" They dashed out of the circus tent and rushed the egg back to the barn.

Circus Shapes

Barney is having a lot of fun playing with the clowns! He wants them to learn more about shapes but he needs your help. Can you help Barney show the clowns a circle? Can you find a star? Well done! There are triangle shapes here also. Can you find them? Thanks for helping the clowns learn more about shapes!

47

Circus Maze

Help Barney and Baby Bop find BJ at the circus.

Clowning Around!

Help Barney find the clown
dressed like him.

Barney Makes A New Friend!

Barney, Baby Bop and BJ race back to the farm with their precious egg. They quickly put it back where they found it just as it begins to hatch! "Wow!" says BJ. "Who can it be?" "I think we're about to meet a new friend," Barney chuckles.

Here's Barney's Friend – Twinken!

Twinken is a dream-maker. He helps children to see their dreams more clearly. And when you see your dream clearly, you can make it come true! What's your dream? What would you like to be when you grow up?

Friends Forever!
by Mark Bernthal

Barney, BJ, and Baby Bop returned the egg to the barn just in time to watch it hatch! They were very happy to see their new friend, Twinken, the dream-maker, break out of the egg and float into Barney's arms.

"Why do they call Twinken 'the dream-maker,' Barney?" asked Baby Bop.

"Because he can help you see your dreams more clearly," answered Barney. Sure enough, in the wink of an eye, Twinken made BJ's dream of playing football seem almost real!

"Wow! Cool!" shouted BJ. "I can score a winning goal someday!"

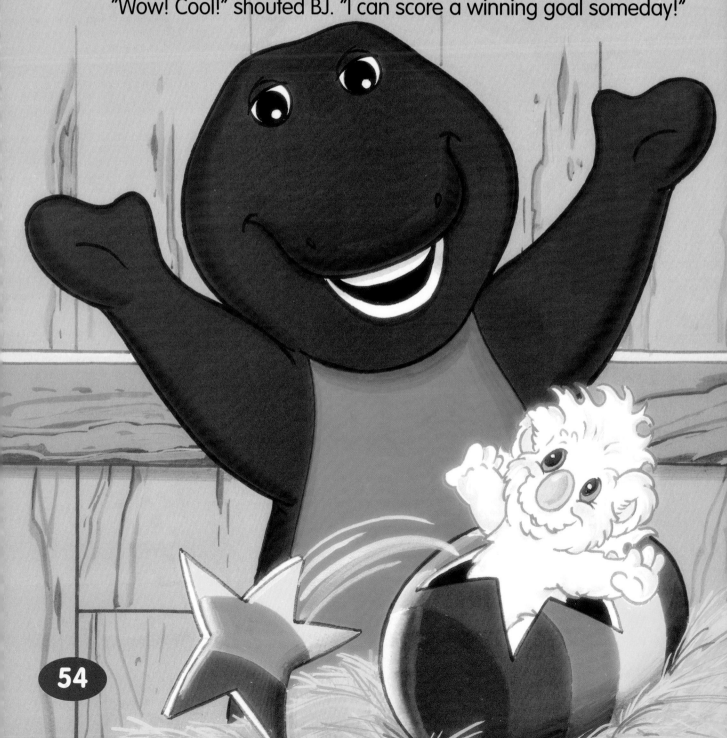

"What about me?" asked Baby Bop. "Can Twinken help me to see my dreams better?"

"Sure," answered Barney with a chuckle, "just watch." Twinken cooed softly, and suddenly, Baby Bop saw herself in a pretty pink ballet tutu, dancing on stage in front of a big audience. "I can't wait to be a ballerina!" said Baby Bop.

"Will Twinken show us your dream, Barney?" asked BJ. With a smile from Twinken, Barney's dream came clearly into view.

"I'm glad we never stopped chasing the egg," said Barney, "because now my dream came true! I can share time with friends I love!" Barney, BJ, Baby Bop, and Twinken will always be friends! Friends forever!

58

Twinkle, Twinkle, Little Twinken!

Help Twinken to find his way through the sky to

Barney and Baby Bop.

"We love you!"